S0-CSY-937

The
SUPERMAN
Book of
SUPERHUMAN
ACHIEVEMENTS

The SUPERMAN® Book of SUPERHUMAN ACHIEVEMENTS

by Shep Steneman

Illustrated by
Ross Andru and Joe Orlando

Random House New York

Photograph credits: The Bettmann Archive, Inc., 20, 22, 29, 56, 71, 88; Black Star, 24; Bruce Coleman, Inc., cover (bottom right), 59; Marc Bulka/Black Star, 60; Robert Burroughs/Black Star, 3; John Coleman/Sygma, cover (top right), 34; Jerry Cooke/"Sports Illustrated," 43, 47 (top), 53, 63; Culver Pictures, Inc., 25, 55; Sally DiMartini © 1980, 23; James Drake/"Sports Illustrated," 44; Graham Finlayson/"Sports Illustrated," 75; © Stephen Green-Armytage/The Image Bank, 1 (right); John Iacono/"Sports Illustrated," 80; Neil Leifer/"Sports Illustrated," 26; National Aeronautics and Space Administration, 16, 18, 19; New York State Commerce Department, 8, 10, 31; Norwegian Information Service, 61; Harold Roth © 1978, 86–87; Mike Sheil/Black Star, 74; Smithsonian Institution, 17, 70, 72; Sovfoto, 30, 73; © John Lewis Stage/The Image Bank, 62; Charlotte Staub, cover (top left), 1 (left); Sygma/Poncet, cover (bottom left), 68; Tony Triolo/"Sports Illustrated," 47, (bottom and right), 48; U.S. Air Force, 37, 82; U.S. Navy, 27; United Press International, 2, 4, 11, 14, 39, 45, 49, 69; Wide World Photos Inc., 5, 9, 12, 13, 15, 21, 28, 32, 35, 36, 38, 40, 41, 42, 46, 50, 51, 54, 57, 65, 66, 67, 78, 79, 81, 84.

 Published in the United States by Random House, Inc., New York, and simultaneously in Canada by Random House of Canada Limited, Toronto.

Library of Congress Cataloging in Publication Data

Steneman, Shep. The Superman book of superhuman achievements. Includes index. Summary: Describes in text and photos the stories behind more than 100 record-breaking achievements. 1. Curiosities and wonders—Juvenile literature. [1. Curiosities and wonders] I. Title.
AG243.S77 031'.02 79-5572
ISBN 0-394-84410-6 AACR2
ISBN 0-394-94410-0 (lib. bdg.)

Manufactured in the United States of America 1 2 3 4 5 6 7 8 9 0

BACKYARD PROJECT

For 33 years Simon Rodia spent all his spare time on a special backyard project in the Watts section of Los Angeles. The Italian immigrant used concrete, seashells, broken dishes, old bottles, and colored tiles to build "towers" that soared into the sky. The tallest tower was 104 feet tall, and Simon Rodia built it and all the others entirely with his own two hands.

After Rodia left Los Angeles in 1954, some people said that the towers were unsafe. City inspectors tested the towers by trying to pull them down with heavy cables. The cables snapped, but the towers stood firm. Rodia's Watts Towers are now considered one of Los Angeles's most fascinating landmarks.

DREAM HOUSE

It took Mr. and Mrs. Elis Stenman of Pigeon Cove, Massachusetts, more than 20 years to build their dream house. When their home was completed, they had a really unique place. From the roof to the walls, the fireplace, and the rocking chair, everything in the house was made up of newspapers—more than 100,000 of them.

BIG YARN

Francis Johnson of Darwin, Minnesota, collects many things. But his prize possession is his collection of twine.

The little ball of string he began saving in 1950 has grown to be the largest in the world. It is 11 feet in diameter, and weighs 5 tons.

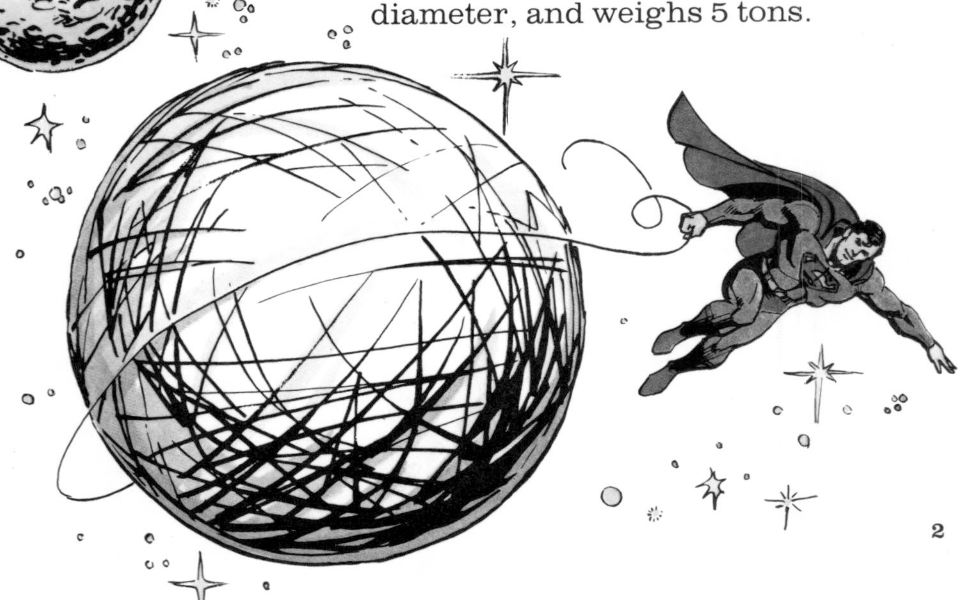

BIG COVER-UP

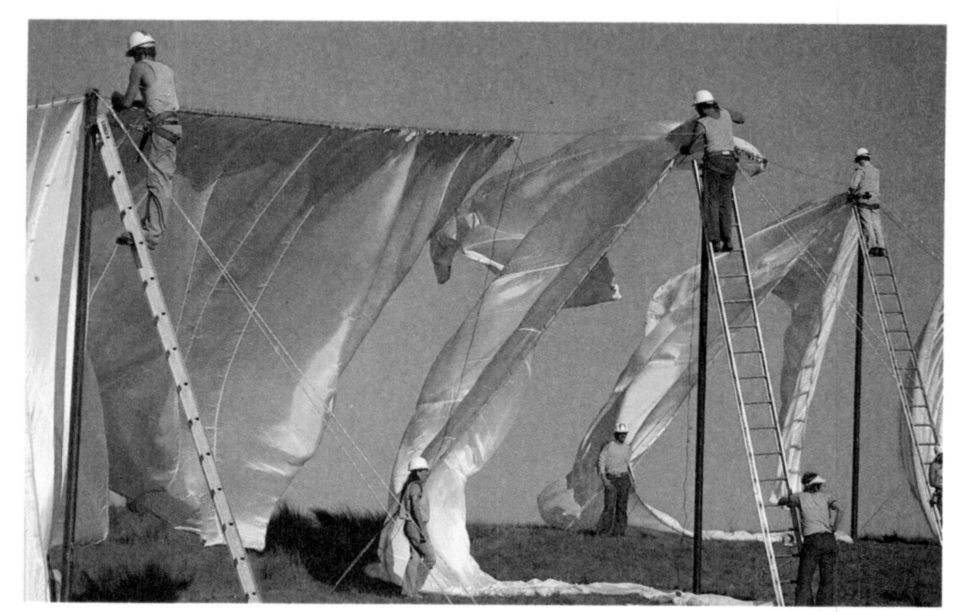

The artist Christo likes to do things in a big way. Early in his career he and his helpers wrapped an entire museum in an enormous tarpaulin.

In 1972 he displayed "Valley Curtain" at Rifle Gap, Colorado. It was the world's largest curtain—more than 1,250 feet wide and 200 feet high. But it lasted only 28 hours after it was hung, because a sandstorm blew it apart.

In September 1976 Christo went to Northern California to create an even bigger work called "Running Fence." The 18-foot-tall white fabric fence wound 24 miles through the countryside. Like "Valley Curtain," it no longer exists. Just as he'd promised, Christo had it taken down only two weeks after it went up.

BIG ORDER

Pizzeria owner Lorenzo Amato celebrated Columbus Day in a big way in 1977. He baked a pizza that measured more than 40 feet across and weighed more than 2 tons. He had to use a "cherry-picker" lift to sprinkle the pepperoni on top.

Amato went on to break his own record in 1978 by constructing a pizza that was 80 feet across. He used 316 gallons of tomato sauce, 1,320 pounds of cheese, and 1,200 pounds of pepperoni to create this masterpiece.

WIENER WINNER

It won't go down in the baseball record books, but on the night of July 12, 1977, baseball fans at Philadelphia's Veterans Stadium saw history in the making. In a pre-game contest, Linda Kuerth gobbled 23 hot dogs in just over 3 minutes.

FAST BALL No major-league pitcher who ever lived could boast of having 110 no-hitters, 35 perfect games, and a fast ball clocked at 118 miles per hour. Not to mention a lifetime batting average over .300. But between 1958 and 1976 one softball pitcher did put these amazing statistics together. Her name is Joan Joyce.

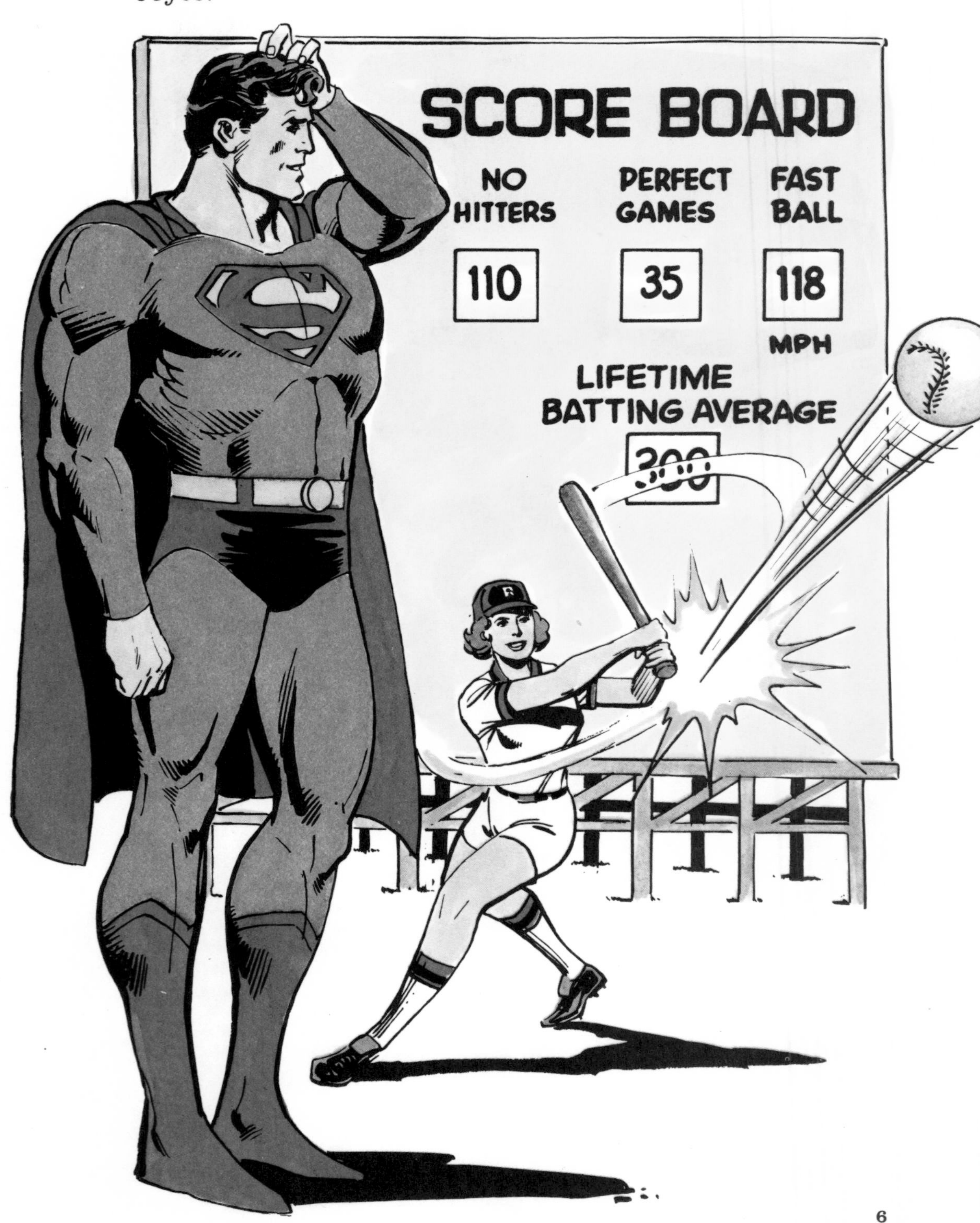

RIP CORD

Georgia Thompson "Tiny" Broadwick made her first parachute jump from a balloon when she was just 15. In 1913 she became the first woman ever to make a parachute jump from an airplane.

A year later her husband invented a special parachute that could be worn like a coat. At that time parachutes were supposed to be pulled open automatically by a cord attached to an airplane. When Tiny was ready to jump, she noticed that somehow the cord had become tangled.

Instead of landing and fixing the cord, Tiny simply cut it in two. The tangled part dropped away. Then she made her jump.

She fell through the air in her unopened chute, becoming the first person to experience "free fall." Once she was clear of the plane, she pulled what was left of her cord (today it is called a rip cord) and her parachute billowed open. Tiny Broadwick landed safely a few minutes later. She had completed the world's first free-fall parachute jump.

BARREL OF FUN

Niagara Falls

A few fearless souls had shot the rapids below Niagara Falls in barrels, but no one had ever survived going over the Falls. That didn't stop Anna Taylor. In 1901 the plucky 43-year-old schoolteacher decided to challenge the Falls. She had a special barrel built that was weighted on the bottom to keep it from tipping over and cushioned on the inside to prevent injuries.

Anna Taylor climbed into the barrel above the Horseshoe Falls on October 24. The barrel was sealed and then pumped full of air. It was then towed out into the rushing current and set free.

The barrel tumbled through swirling rock-filled waters and hurtled on toward the Falls. Thousands of people held their breath as they saw the barrel plummet over the edge into the churning water below.

It took 15 minutes for boatmen downstream to catch up with the bobbing barrel. They quickly opened it. Mrs. Taylor had survived!

Her scalp had been cut, and her back and shoulders ached, but she was still lively enough to wave to the crowd. Later she told them not to try to repeat "the foolish thing I have done."

WALKING THE LINE

In the summer of 1859 a French acrobat who called himself Blondin strung a rope across the gorge just below Niagara Falls. On June 30 he was ready to walk across that rope from the United States to Canada—more than 150 feet above Niagara's violent waters.

Blondin sat down on the rope halfway across. The crowd gasped as he lowered a string to a boat below, pulled up a bottle, and took a drink. Then he continued his terrifying walk. Eighteen minutes after he began his stroll, he was greeted by tremendous cheers as he stepped onto the Canadian side. It took him less than 7 minutes to make the quarter-mile return trip to America.

Many people came to the Falls that summer to see what the acrobat would do next. Blondin didn't disappoint them. He walked across with a sack over his head. He held out his hat and let a marksman shoot it from below! He pushed a wheelbarrow across! He did a headstand on the rope!

Somehow he convinced his manager, Harry Colcord, to ride across on his back. That trip didn't go as smoothly as the others. A support wire snapped, jerking the main rope sideways, but Blondin managed to keep himself and his passenger from falling. After 45 agonizing minutes, the two landed safely on the other side.

At various times, Blondin went across at night, on stilts, backward, and in chains. Once he even took a table, chair, and stove with him to the middle of the rope, fixed an omelet, and sat down for a snack. Blondin became the most famous daredevil of his time.

STRAIGHT AND NARROW

On August 7, 1974, Philippe Petit strolled back and forth on a 131-foot cable strung between the tops of the twin towers of the World Trade Center in New York City. The tightrope was more than 1,350 feet high.

Petit and his friends had secretly put the cable up the night before. Shortly after dawn the French acrobat went out onto the quarter-mile-high cable. He did knee bends and other stunts for 45 minutes.

When asked why he had done it, Petit said, "If I see three oranges, I have to juggle. And if I see two towers, I have to walk."

CROSS OVER THE BRIDGE

Verrazano-Narrows Bridge

Engineer Othmar H. Ammann was one of the world's greatest bridge designers. He designed the George Washington Bridge that crosses the Hudson River between New York City and New Jersey. When it opened in 1931, it was by far the longest suspension bridge ever built.

Ammann worked on many bridges after that. But his greatest achievement was the 6,690-foot Verrazano-Narrows Bridge that stretches between Brooklyn and Staten Island in New York City. The cables that support the roadway are made up of more than 145,000 miles of wire. That's enough wire to go around the world nearly five times! The steel in each of the 690-foot-tall main towers is held together by more than 4,000,000 bolts and rivets.

The Verrazano-Narrows Bridge is so long that the two main towers are 1⅝ inches farther apart at the top than at the bottom—to allow for the curvature of the earth. When the bridge opened in November 1964, its center span was the longest of any suspension bridge on earth.

CHANNEL CHALLENGE

Gertrude Ederle before her Channel swim

The English Channel stretches 21 miles between England and France. The Channel's treacherous currents and icy waters have challenged long-distance swimmers for more than 100 years. An Englishman named Matthew Webb made the first cross-channel swim in 1875. By 1926, four other men had accomplished the dangerous feat.

In 1925 an 18-year old New Yorker named Gertrude Ederle tried to make the crossing—and failed. A year later on August 6, 1926, she tried again. She was coated with grease to protect her from the cold water. She plunged into the Channel at 7:09 a.m. to begin her long swim to England.

Trudy was only halfway across when a storm began to rage. Fierce currents and high waves threatened to tire her, but she refused to give up.

The crowd waiting on the English coast began to cheer as they saw Trudy in the distance. People waded out to meet her, and wrapped her in blankets as she stumbled to her feet.

Gertrude Ederle was the first woman to swim the English Channel. She had done it in 14 hours and 31 minutes—nearly 2 hours quicker than the fastest man's time.

BETTER THE SECOND TIME

Cynthia Nicholas, a 19-year-old student from Ontario, Canada, swam the English Channel from Dover, England, to the coast of France in 1977 in just under 9 hours. Nicholas had enough energy and stamina to turn around and swim back to England. She was the fifth person—and the first woman—to make the round-trip swim. And she did it in the record time of 19 hours and 55 minutes. That was more than 10 hours faster than the previous record.

NO JOKE

It took Hugo Vihlen 85 days to sail the Atlantic Ocean from Casablanca, Morocco, to Florida in 1968. That was because his sailboat, the "April Fool," was so small—just under 6 feet long. It was the smallest craft to cross the Atlantic.

ACROSS THE ICE

Expeditions have been made to the North Pole by dogsled, airplane, airship, submarine, icebreaker, and snowmobile. But no one had ever made this dangerous journey alone.

Japanese explorer Naomi Uemura wanted to be the first. He headed north from Canada's Cape Columbia March 5, 1978, with a team of dogs and a sled loaded with half a ton of provisions. During his journey he was scheduled to receive five airlifts of food and supplies. The rest of the time he would be entirely on his own.

An attacking polar bear nearly put an end to his expedition only 4 days after it had begun. Uemura had to hack his way through ice ridges nearly 30 feet tall, with temperatures as low as -38 degrees Celsius. Later, as temperatures rose, cracks in the ice became a problem. Uemura had to reach for ice blocks he could use as bridges across the open water. On April 29, after 55 days and 600 miles of travel, Naomi Uemura reached the North Pole. He had done what few men had done before him—and he had done it alone.

EVERREST CONQUERED

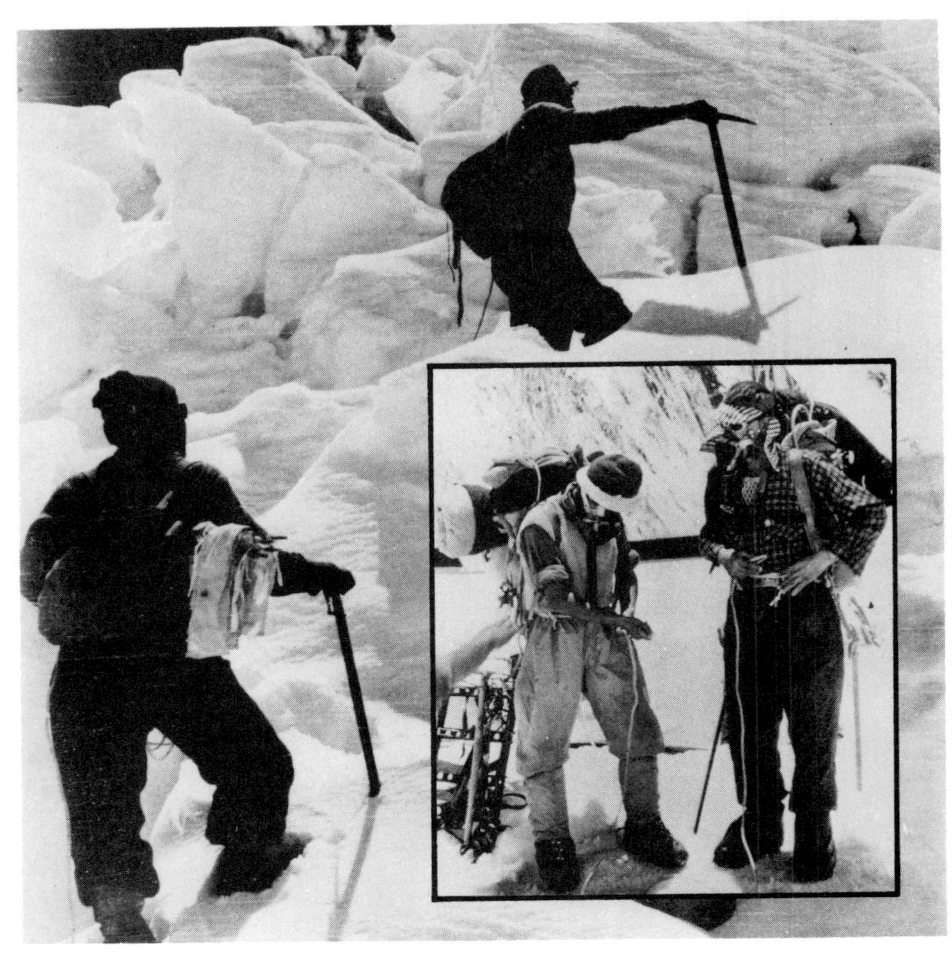

Tenzing Norgay (left) and Edmund Hillary

Mountaineer Edmund Hillary of New Zealand joined a British expedition in 1953 that was headed for the top of Mount Everest, 5½ miles above sea level.

The British team moved into the Himalayan mountains of Nepal in early April. Tenzing Norgay, the greatest of the native Sherpa guides, joined the team. At one point in the expedition, the Sherpa saved Hillary's life when some thin ice broke under his weight.

As the climb progressed, the going got rougher and some of the climbers couldn't continue. The cold became fierce, and the air was so thin that the climbers had to wear oxygen masks. Even the leader of the expedition had to turn back. Only Tenzing Norgay and Edmund Hillary were able to keep climbing.

Their oxygen was running low on May 29, but Hillary and Norgay made one last attempt to reach the top. They pulled themselves over a huge boulder, and climbed across ridges until there was nowhere else to climb. Finally, at 11:30 a.m. that day, Edmund Hillary and Tenzing Norgay reached their goal—the top of the world.

TOP OF THE TOWN

George Willig climbs as police follow.

Each of the twin towers of New York's World Trade Center is 1,350 feet high. At 6:30 a.m. on May 26, 1977, George Willig began climbing up the side of the South Tower on his long way to the top.

Willig used nylon rope and special clamps that fit into the tracks of the window-washing machines. Policemen tried to persuade him to stop his climb, but Willig just kept going. Traffic stopped. A crowd below watched in amazement as he neared the top.

At 10:05 a.m. Willig finally reached the roof of the tower. He had set a record for distance climbing up the outside of a building. "It was a personal challenge, a challenge to my ingenuity," Willig said afterward. "I just wanted the prize of getting to the top."

New York's citizens hailed Willig as a hero, but city officials didn't agree. They sued him for $250,000 for all the trouble and expense he had caused.

The next day the case was settled out of court. Willig paid the city a fine of $1.10. That was one cent for each of the 110 stories he had climbed.

MAN ON THE MOON

Neil Armstrong (left) and Edwin Aldrin raise American flag.

Alan Shepard was the first American astronaut to be rocketed into space. Though his ride lasted only a few minutes, he was a national hero. But even then, many people were looking to the future. President John F. Kennedy told Congress that the United States should work toward landing a man on the moon before the 1960s ended. It seemed an impossible dream.

But 8 years and many space flights later, the dream came true. The lunar lander "Eagle" touched down on the moon on July 20, 1969. At 10:56 that night astronaut Neil Armstrong came down the Eagle's ladder in his space suit and set foot on the lunar surface. A quarter of a million miles away, television sets and radios brought people around the world his historic words: "That's one small step for a man, one giant leap for mankind."

Edwin "Buzz" Aldrin came out of the "Eagle" to join Armstrong 20 minutes later. They took photographs, collected soil samples, and learned how to walk in the moon's low gravity during the 2 hours they were the men on the moon. The first mission to the moon was a success. The "Eagle" had landed.

ROCKET POWER

Even when he was a small boy, Dr. Robert Goddard was fascinated with the idea of sending rockets into space. But most people considered such travel impossible. Signal flares and fireworks were the only rockets that had ever flown, and they had traveled into the air only a few hundred feet.

Many laughed at Goddard, but he paid no attention. In 1914 he patented some basic principles of modern rocketry. His multi-stage design, with each stage dropping away when its fuel supply is used up, is still in use today. So are many of his other ideas.

Goddard later began designing and building his own rockets, including the first liquid-fueled rocket. Even though none of Goddard's rockets ever made it into space, every modern space flight owes much of its success to his pioneering experiments.

BY JUPITER!

Volcano erupts on Io, one of Jupiter's moons.

In 1610 Italian astronomer Galileo Galilei became the first person ever to see any of the moons of the planet Jupiter. Galileo observed four of them by using a telescope he had built himself. The moons looked like tiny bright dots.

Telescopes grew larger and more powerful over the next three and a half centuries. They revealed more and more about the universe. More moons of Jupiter were sighted. But many mysteries still remained. It wasn't until 1975 that astronomers discovered Jupiter's thirteenth moon.

In 1979 the American spacecraft "Voyager I" passed within 175,000 miles of Jupiter's surface. "Voyager's" cameras transmitted to Earth the first close-up color pictures of Jupiter and its moons. Scientists studied these pictures and discovered Jupiter's fourteenth moon, as well as a faint ring around the planet.

Space probes like "Voyager" give scientists a better understanding of the universe. Further probes will help unlock even more of the secrets of the cosmos.

RADIO STARS

Radio telescope at Arecibo, Puerto Rico

An engineer named Karl Jansky discovered in the early 1930s that faint radio signals were coming from distant stars. Professional astronomers didn't pay much attention to him.

But a radio expert named Grote Reber wanted to hear the radio signals. In October 1938 he designed a special 30-foot dish-shaped antenna and built it in his backyard. He began to pick up signals from the stars. Today astronomers all over the world use similar instruments to pick up signals from galaxies that are so far away that they can't even be photographed. Grote Reber had built the world's first radio telescope in his own backyard.

MECHANICAL WIZARD

Thomas Edison, one of the greatest inventors in history, came up with improvements in the motion-picture camera, the storage battery, the telephone, and the light bulb. But one of Edison's cleverest inventions was the phonograph.

He came up with the idea in 1877 and sketched plans so that an assistant could build a working model. When the assistant brought him the new instrument, Edison put a piece of tinfoil in it. He lowered a needle onto the foil, turned a crank, and recited the words "Mary had a little lamb."

Edison then moved the needle back to the starting position and turned the crank again. He and his assistants were thrilled to hear Edison's voice coming from the machine. Thomas Edison's recital of a nursery rhyme was the world's first phonograph recording.

THE VOICE SOUNDS FAMILIAR

Jane Barbe of Atlanta, Georgia, talks to more people over the telephone than anyone else in the world. Mrs. Barbe records time, temperature, and other messages for phone companies in over 450 American and Canadian cities. Millions of people hear her familiar voice every day.

HEAVY NEWS

When Jackie Jones of Lindale, Texas, wrote to her sister, she didn't leave out one bit of news. Mrs. Jean Stewart of Prentiss, Maine, received Jackie's handwritten letter in the mail. It was 318 feet long, weighed 15 pounds, and contained more than 1,000,000 words.

WHAT'S IN A NAME?

You might think you'd have a big crowd if you invited to dinner Martin Clifford, Harry Clifton, Clifford Clive, Sir Alan Cobham, Owen Conquest, Gordon Conway, Harry Dorian, Frank Drake, Freeman Fox, Hamilton Greening, Cecil Herber, Prosper Howard, Robert Jennings, Gillingham Jones, T. Harcourt Llewelyn, Clifford Owen, Ralph Redway, Ridley Redway, Frank Richards, Hilda Richards, Raleigh Robbins, Robert Rogers, Eric Stanhope, Robert Stanley, Nigel Wallace, and Talbot Wynyard. But they'd all have been able to sit in the same chair. That's because these people were the same person. All these pen names were used by a writer whose real name was Charles Harold St. John Hamilton. Hamilton wrote more than 5,000 stories for children between 1906 and 1940. It's been estimated that he wrote over 100,000,000 words during his lifetime.

TRANSLATOR'S KEY

The Rosetta Stone

The meaning of ancient Egyptian writing puzzled scholars for a long time. Translators needed a key to unlock the mystery.

In 1798 in Rosetta, Egypt, French soldiers found a stone that had three different kinds of inscriptions—one in Greek and two in ancient Egyptian writings. All three messages appeared to say the same thing. The Greek was easy to translate, and it seemed that the Egyptian writings could be translated by using the Greek as a "key." But no one could solve the puzzle.

In 1818, 28-year-old Jean François Champollion discovered that in the Egyptian writing called hieroglyphics, some pictures stand for sounds. By 1822, the French scholar had solved the mystery of language that had baffled experts for so long. The Rosetta Stone could be read. But Champollion did not receive credit for his stunning achievement until 30 years after his death.

NEW ALPHABET

Child reading a Braille book

Louis Braille was born in a small French village in 1809. He was only 3 years old when he lost his sight in an accident. He was sent to a special school for blind children in Paris when he was 10. There he was taught to use his fingers to read special books that were printed in raised letters. But it was not easy to tell one letter from another.

Then he learned about a writing system a military man had invented so that soldiers could read messages in the dark. The system used raised dots that were punched into paper. The dots stood for different sounds. The dots were a good idea, but the system wasn't. There were too many symbols to remember.

Louis Braille decided to develop his own system of writing with raised dots. He worked on the problem for 3 years. When he was 15 years old, he discovered a simple way to make a raised-dot alphabet.

Braille's fellow students liked his alphabet idea, but educational authorities refused to accept it. After a public demonstration of its use in 1844, the raised-dot alphabet became more popular. It was named Braille, after its inventor, and it is still the written language of the blind today.

LITTLE STEVIE

Steveland Morris was born blind. He taught himself to play the harmonica at a very young age. Then he learned to play other instruments and began writing his own songs.

When he was only 12 years old, he recorded "Fingertips" under the name Little Stevie Wonder. The recording soon became America's number-one hit. It sold more than a 1,000,000 copies, making it a "gold record." Young Stevie Wonder was a star.

At 21, Stevie Wonder had earned over $1,000,000 from his many hits. Now he began producing albums that were truly his own. He wrote and sang all the songs himself. He usually played all the instruments—everything from drums and harmonica to piano and electronic synthesizer. These records were even more successful than any he had made before.

In 1974 Stevie Wonder won 5 Grammy awards, more than anyone else had ever received in a single year. In 1975 he earned 5 more. But Stevie Wonder wasn't satisfied just winning awards. In 1979 he wrote the sound track for a motion picture. It was one more remarkable achievement for this amazing musician.

RICH "KID"

Jackie Coogan (right) with Charlie Chaplin

Jackie Coogan was one of the biggest stars in the silent movies. He was only 5 years old when he appeared in "The Kid" with Charlie Chaplin in 1920. By the time he turned 7, he had earned more than $1,000,000 as a film star. Jackie Coogan was probably the youngest self-made millionaire in history.

GOLDEN GIRL

Marjorie Gestring of the United States was the youngest person ever to win an individual Olympic gold medal. When she became springboard-diving champion in 1936, Marjorie was only 13 years old.

SOLID GOLD SWIMMER

On August 28, 1972, in Munich, Germany, Mark Spitz sprang into the Olympic pool and sped to a new world record for the 200-meter butterfly. It was his first individual Olympic gold medal.

Half an hour later he swam the final leg of the 400-meter freestyle relay. The American team easily defeated the second-place Russians, and Mark Spitz earned his second Olympic gold that year.

On August 29, Spitz came from behind in the 200-meter freestyle to capture another world record—and still another gold medal. In the 100-yard butterfly Spitz again splashed home in world record time. He was the anchorman for the 800-meter relay and won one more gold medal in another record breaker. On September 3, he captured the 100-meter freestyle gold.

The next day he swam the butterfly in the 400-meter medley relay. By the time he finished his swim, he had given the American team a 12-foot lead and another world record.

Mark Spitz had won an astounding seventh gold medal. No athlete before or since has ever won so many gold medals or been a part of so many world-record performances in one Olympic Games.

DEEP DIVE

In the 1940s Swiss scientist Auguste Piccard invented the deep-sea diving vessel called the bathyscaphe. But it was on January 23, 1960, that his own son gave it the ultimate test.

At 8:23 a.m. that day Jacques Piccard and U.S. Navy Lieutenant Donald Walsh climbed into the bathyscaphe "Trieste" and sealed it shut. Their goal lay nearly 7 miles below. They wanted to reach the bottom of the Marianas Trench, the deepest known spot in the Pacific Ocean.

The "Trieste" was lowered into the water and slowly began its descent. Before noon it had reached a depth greater than the height of Mount Everest. Under the tremendous water pressure—nearly 8 tons per square inch—one small outside window cracked, but Piccard and Walsh kept going. At 1:06 p.m. they touched bottom: 35,800 feet below the surface of the sea.

For 20 minutes they were able to observe the fish that swam into the paths of the bathyscaphe lights. Then they began their long trip back. At 4:56 p.m. the "Trieste" broke through the ocean's surface. Jacques Piccard and Donald Walsh had conquered the ocean's greatest depth.

HIGH LIVING

Frank Perkins climbed up a 50-foot pole above a car lot on June 1, 1975, as a publicity stunt. For the next 399 days, the 19-year-old lived in a 4-by-8-foot room on top of the pole. He finally came down on July 4, 1976. The car dealer had gone out of business!

DIET DAYS

For how long can a person miss meals? Angus Barbieri did it for 382 days in a hospital in Dundee, Scotland. He followed a diet of water, coffee, tea, and vitamins and lost nearly 300 pounds between June 1965 and July 1966.

POLES APART

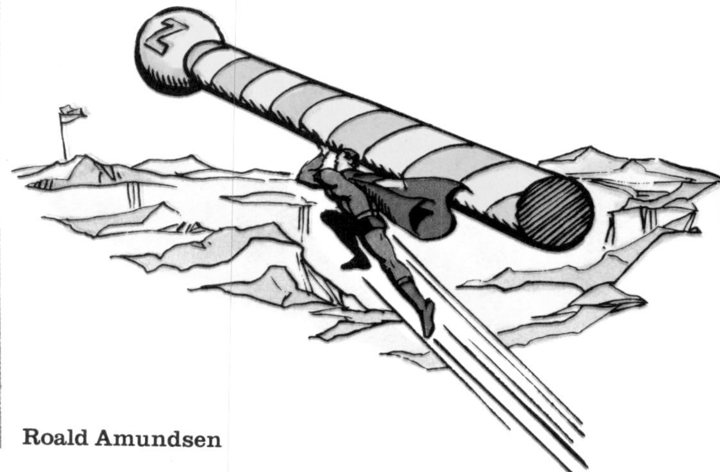

Roald Amundsen

Norwegian explorer Roald Amundsen had hoped to be the first person to reach the North Pole. But in 1909 he learned of American Robert Peary's claim that he had already arrived at the Pole.

Although Amundsen saw no point in being second, he still continued his preparations for a polar expedition. What he kept secret, even from his crew, was that he'd changed his destination to the South Pole. One reason for the secrecy was that Great Britain's Captain Robert Scott was aiming for the same target.

In January 1911 (the height of the Antarctic summer) Amundsen's party made camp on the Antarctic ice. They set up stockpiles of food and supplies along their route to the Pole. Then they settled down for the six-month darkness of the Antarctic winter.

After one false start in weather so bitterly cold it killed some of their sled dogs, Amundsen and his men left for the Pole on October 20. Terrible weather struck again, but they continued their journey. After traveling a month across glaciers and frozen mountains, they had to shoot two dozen of their weakest sled dogs and use them for meat.

On December 8 they penetrated farther south than any human had ever been before. At last, on December 14, Amundsen and his men reached the Pole and planted their flag in the ice.

When Scott's expedition reached the spot a month later, they had to face the disappointment of finding the Norwegian flag there to greet them. Roald Amundsen and his men had won the race to the South Pole.

OUT OF THIS WORLD

Both dogs and chimpanzees had been sent into space and brought back safely by 1961. But scientists were not sure just what effect space flight would have on a human being. After months of intensive training, Russian cosmonaut Yuri Gagarin was the first to find out. On April 12, 1961, at 9:07 a.m. the rockets beneath his "Vostok I" capsule blasted him into space.

Gagarin orbited at a speed of nearly 18,000 miles per hour, 200 miles above the earth. This was more than five times faster and farther from the planet than any human had ever traveled. During his hour and a half flight, he was fascinated by the sensation of weightlessness. No one else had ever been free from earth's gravity for more than a few seconds at a time. And no one else had ever seen so much of the earth at one time.

After spending nearly 2 hours in space, "Vostok I" touched down on a Russian field. Two days later Yuri Gagarin was given his country's highest honors in a ceremony in Moscow. Huge crowds gathered to cheer a hero—the world's first man in space.

GOING UP

In his 1933 film King Kong climbed up the outside of New York's Empire State Building, with the help of some movie magic. Almost everyone else takes the elevators. But in a special contest, runners raced up the 1,575 stairs to the observation deck on the eighty-sixth floor.

Running up stairs takes a lot more effort than running on a level course. Although the Empire State "run up" is only 1,050 feet, the best effort so far has been Jim Rafferty's 1979 record time of 12 minutes and 19.8 seconds. That's more than ten times longer than it would take a good runner to cover the same distance on a track. After his record-breaking performance, Rafferty and his fellow contestants took the elevators down!

BACKWARD, MARCH!

Plennie L. Wingo set out in 1931 to walk around the world—backward. Using special rear-view glasses, he crossed the United States and Europe. But when he got to Istanbul, Turkey, the police refused to let him continue. By that time he had already set the world's backward-walking distance record. Wingo claimed that he had fallen only once in all his reverse traveling.

In 1976 he took his special glasses out of retirement and began another backward hike. The backward champion successfully walked more than 400 miles between San Francisco and Santa Monica, California—at the age of 81.

OLYMPIC FEET

Scarlet fever and pneumonia left 4-year-old Wilma Rudolph unable to walk properly. Since she didn't want to let her eighteen brothers and sisters always beat her to the dinner table, she kept on doing the exercises that were supposed to make her stronger.

By the time she was in her teens, she had no trouble walking. In fact, she had developed into a terrific runner. At 16, she won a bronze medal at the 1956 Olympics as a member of the United States relay team.

Her greatest performance came at the 1960 Olympics in Rome. She won gold medals by wide margins in the 100-meter and 200-meter races. Then she made up the time her slower teammates had lost in the 400-meter relay and came from behind to win the race for the United States. In 1960 Wilma Rudolph was the world's fastest woman runner.

CROSS-COUNTRY RACE

The "Bunion Derby" started on March 4, 1928. One hundred ninety-nine runners lined up in Los Angeles for the start of the first coast-to-coast foot race in history.

Fifty-five of the runners got as far as Ohio. Finally, 84 days and 3,422 miles after he'd begun, an Oklahoma farmboy named Andy Payne was declared the winner at New York's Madison Square Garden. He had crossed the continent in a running time of 573 hours, 4 minutes, and 3 seconds.

MAN ON THE RUN

If there's a record for wearing out shoes, Max Telford might be just the one to set it. That's because he has run more than 100,000 miles. In 1977 the 42-year-old Telford ran nonstop for more than 31½ hours, covering a distance of 186 miles.

And that was just a warm-up. Later that year, he went to Anchorage, Alaska, to begin a running trip across North America. One hundred eight days and 5,110 miles later, he wound up his journey in Halifax, Nova Scotia.

FASTEST MAN ON EARTH

At Utah's Bonneville Salt Flats on September 9, 1979, a Hollywood stunt man named Stan Barrett drove a 48,000-horsepower rocket car to a world land-speed record of 638.637 miles per hour. It wasn't a smooth ride. The car bounced and vibrated so much that the rear became airborne for nearly a hundred feet at a time.

On December 17 Barrett drove the same car on a dry lake bed in California. He bettered his old record by more than 100 miles an hour and became the first person to go faster than the speed of sound on land.

TWO-WHEELED LIGHTNING

A streamliner is a special kind of motorcycle that's built for just one thing—speed.

In September 1975 at Utah's Bonneville Salt Flats, motorcyclist Don Vesco squeezed into his red and yellow streamliner, "Silver Bird," and broke one speed record after another. On September 28 he was determined to shatter the 300-mile-an-hour barrier.

With a 5-mile head start, Vesco shot through the 1-mile timing trap twice at an average speed of 302.9 miles per hour. His best run was clocked at nearly 308 miles per hour.

Don Vesco had become the fastest person on two wheels.

FOUR-WHEEL WONDER

John Hutson crouched low on his aluminum skateboard at Signal Hill, California, in June 1978. When the competition began, he sped at nearly 40 miles an hour down the steep slope of Hill Street. His speed kept building until he reached the bottom. Then he went back to the top for a second try. Both of his 600-yard runs were timed at exactly the same world-record speed—53.45 miles per hour.

FOUR-MINUTE BARRIER

During the early 1900s it seemed impossible that anyone could run a mile in less than 4 minutes. The fastest time clocked was 4 minutes and 15 seconds. Even as late as 1923, the world's best runners could do no better than 4 minutes and 10 seconds. In 1945 a Swede named Gunder Haegg took the record down to 4 minutes and 1.4 seconds.

On May 6, 1954, a British medical student named Roger Bannister crouched in the starting area on a track near Oxford. The weather was miserable and blustery, but Bannister was determined to break the world mile record that day. His Oxford teammates set a lightning pace for the first three-quarters of a mile. Then Bannister moved forward and took the lead.

As he crossed the finish line, the judges' watches recorded the winning time. The announcement came: "The time for Roger Bannister, three minutes..."

Loud cheers drowned out the rest. The seconds were unimportant. Roger Bannister had broken the 4-minute barrier.

The fastest speed for a winged aircraft was clocked by Major William J. Knight. He piloted an X-15 rocket plane in 1967 to a speed of 4,534 miles per hour. That is nearly seven times the speed of sound. The plane was going so fast that the friction of the air rushing past the plane scorched the wings and burned a hole in the tail.

THE "BABE"

Mildred "Babe" Didrikson was one of the world's greatest all-around athletes. She led her basketball team to a national championship in 1931. She set world records at the 1932 Olympics in the javelin throw and the 80-meter hurdles. And she went on to win every important women's golf tournament, including an amazing 17 in a row in 1946 and 1947.

But her greatest single performance was at the 1932 national track-and-field championships in Evanston, Illinois. Babe competed as a one-woman "team" against the best teams of female athletes in the country. She entered eight events and won five of them. She gave world-record performances in the baseball throw, javelin, and 80-meter hurdles, and matched a previous record in the high jump.

When the team scores were tallied up that day, the runner-up team of 22 women had a total of 22 points. The winning "team," named Babe Didrikson, had 30.

BORING RACE

At the 1952 Olympic Games in Helsinki, Finland, Czechoslovakian long-distance runner Emil Zatopek shaved half a minute off his own Olympic record in the 10,000-meter run. But he said that he was a little disappointed in his time.

He made up for it in the 5,000-meter race by coming from behind to set another Olympic record. Then he announced he would compete in the marathon.

Zatopek had never run the grueling 26-mile race in his life. No one expected him to win. But the amazing Czech finished 2 minutes ahead of the rest of the pack—and 6 minutes ahead of the old Olympic record.

Zatopek still wasn't satisfied. "The marathon," he complained, "is a very boring race."

2 + 2 = 3

In 1909 two athletic coaches teamed up and set a record for the three-legged race that is still unbeaten. Harry Hillman and Lawson Robertson ran 100 yards in 11 seconds flat.

GOAL!

Say the word "soccer," and immediately Pelé comes to mind. Pelé (his real name is Edson Arantes do Nascimento) was born in Brazil. He was a professional soccer player by the time he was 15. At 17, he scored more goals than any other player in Brazil and was named the country's soccer player of the year. This is quite an honor in a country where soccer is the most popular sport.

Pelé played in his first World Cup competition in 1958. He had injured his knee a few weeks earlier, but still led the Brazilian team to victory. In 1962 he again triumphed over injury, helping Brazil to win its second straight World Cup.

In 1969 Pelé became the first soccer player to score 1,000 goals in his career. Then he took Brazil's team to another World Cup victory in 1972. This was the first time any country had become a three-time winner.

Pelé left Brazil in 1975 and joined the New York Cosmos. The fans loved him, and his fantastic style helped make soccer popular in the United States. When he finally retired in 1977, he had a career total of 1,281 goals—the most in soccer history.

CHECKMATE

Bobby Fischer (right) and Boris Spassky study their next moves.

Bobby Fischer was already playing chess at the age of 6. Before he turned 15, he had won two United States championships. At 16, he became the youngest grand master in chess history. In 1972 Fischer challenged Boris Spassky, the world champion from Russia, in Reykjavik, Iceland. Although Fischer lost the first two games, he soon began to win. Bobby Fischer went on to become the first American player to win the world championship of chess.

Al Oerter threw the discus nearly 185 feet for a new Olympic record and a gold medal in 1956. Four years later he broke his own record—and took home another gold medal.

In 1964 he went to the Tokyo Olympics to defend his title. But during practice he tore cartilage in his rib cage. Doctors had to tape his ribs. They packed the area with ice to ease the pain. It looked as though Oerter's reign as Olympic discus champion was over.

Taped and hurting, Oerter went to the stadium for the finals and made 4 bad throws. But on his fifth try he sailed the discus 5 feet farther than he'd ever thrown it before. It was another Olympic record.

Oerter trained hard for the 1968 games. Rain had made the throwing circle muddy and slippery for the finals, and good throws seemed impossible. Al Oerter adjusted his style to allow for the mud and sent the 4½-pound disc flying 212½ feet. This throw earned him a fourth straight Olympic record and gold medal. No one else has ever won a single Olympic event four times in a row over a period of 12 years. Al Oerter meant it when he said, "I just get fired up for the Olympics."

TWO-TIME WINNER

1976 was a big year for American ice skater Sheila Young. She took a gold medal with a record time in the 500-meter sprint at the Innsbruck Olympics. She went on to win the world speed-skating championship later that year.

Then Young turned her talents to cycling. At the National Bicycle Track Championship, she took both the American and world titles. Sheila Young became the first athlete to become world champion in two entirely different sports at the same time.

CHAMPION OF CHAMPIONS

Bruce Jenner didn't win a decathlon medal at the 1972 Olympics. But he promised himself that he would win it the next time. For the next four years he totally devoted himself to rigorous and intensive training for the 10 decathlon events. When Jenner arrived in Montreal for the 1976 Olympics, he already held the current world decathlon record.

In four of the first nine events he did better than he had ever done in his life, and in two others he tied his personal best marks. In the last event, the 1500-meter run, he finished the race in his fastest time ever—and topped his own world decathlon record by 94 points. Bruce Jenner had become the new Olympic decathlon champion.

HOP, STEP, JUMP

Young Ray Ewry was paralyzed by polio. His doctors didn't know if he'd ever be able to walk properly again. They just hoped the leg exercises they recommended would do him some good.

The doctors never dreamed how well their prescription would work. By the time he reached adulthood, Ray Ewry was the number-one jumper in the world.

Ewry specialized in three events that have since been dropped from Olympic competition: the standing high jump; the standing long jump; and the standing hop, step, and jump. He won gold medals in all three events at the Olympics of 1900 and 1904. After that, the hop, step, and jump was discontinued, so Ewry had to settle for only two golds in 1906 and 1908.

Ten wins in ten tries: Ray Ewry's once-crippled legs brought him more individual gold medals than anyone else has ever won in Olympic competition.

DUSK-TO-DAWN DISCO

Need a disco dancer who just won't quit? Send in a marine!

In August 1979 Lance Corporal J. C. Stare started dancing at a New York hotel to help raise money for the Muscular Dystrophy Association. He didn't stop until he'd danced for an unbelievable 332 hours.

PERPETUAL MOTION

Richard John Knecht was 8 years old when he set a world's record for sit-ups. On December 22, 1972, he did 25,222 sit-ups in 11 hours and 14 minutes.

THE PERFECT TEN

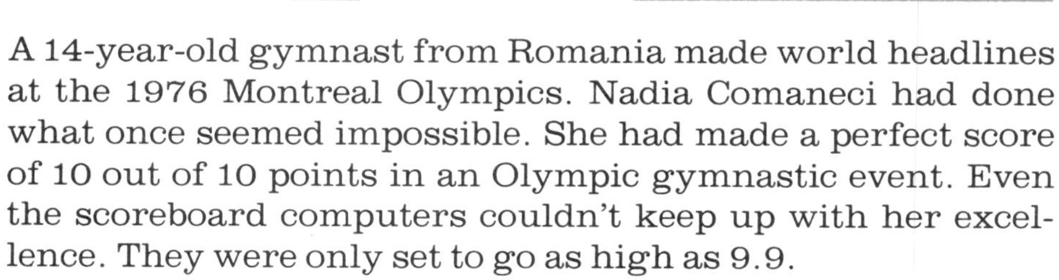

A 14-year-old gymnast from Romania made world headlines at the 1976 Montreal Olympics. Nadia Comaneci had done what once seemed impossible. She had made a perfect score of 10 out of 10 points in an Olympic gymnastic event. Even the scoreboard computers couldn't keep up with her excellence. They were only set to go as high as 9.9.

Nadia kept on giving flawless performances during the Olympic competition. She scored three more 10's on the uneven bars and then three on the balance beam, winning the gold medal in each event. She won a bronze medal for her floor-exercise routine. Her record-breaking overall score gave Nadia a third gold medal—as best all-around woman gymnast.

RIGHT ON TARGET

Target distance didn't seem to be a problem for 19-year-old archer Darrell Pace of the United States. In 1976 his bow and arrow set new Olympic records at 90, 70, 50, and 30 meters.

MAN FOR ALL SEASONS

Winning 1932 U.S. bobsled team

Eddie Eagen won his first Olympic gold medal at the 1920 Olympics as a light-heavyweight boxer. Twelve years later at the Winter Olympics, he won a second gold medal as a member of America's four-man bobsled team. That made Eddie Eagen the only person to ever win gold medals at both Summer and Winter Olympic Games.

SLUGGER JOE

New York Yankee outfielder Joe DiMaggio hit a single on May 15, 1941, that began a hitting streak many baseball experts consider untouchable. For the next two months DiMaggio got at least one hit in every game.

Finally, on the night of July 17, two Cleveland pitchers were able to stop him. But Joe DiMaggio had hit safely in 56 straight games—12 more than anyone else had done before or has done since.

"THE GREATEST"

Muhammad Ali (left) on his way to victory over Leon Spinks

Muhammad Ali won the world heavyweight boxing championship once, lost it, and won it back again. He lost the title once more in February 1978 in a fight with Leon Spinks. Many people thought it was time for Ali to retire from boxing.

But Ali had different ideas. He scheduled a rematch with Spinks and trained hard for the chance to recapture his title. On September 15, 1978, Ali jabbed, danced, clinched, and punched his way to a unanimous decision over Spinks. "The Greatest" had won his third heavyweight championship—something no other fighter had ever accomplished before.

BIG HEART

Many people give of themselves to help others, but Philadelphia strongman Edward "Spike" Howard gave more than most people. During his life, Howard donated an estimated 1,056 pints of blood to patients who desperately needed it.

Spike Howard got his nickname from his vaudeville trick of bending spikes with his bare hands. He once pulled a 15-ton fire truck 100 feet with his teeth. But the achievement Spike was proudest of was his record for giving blood.

UPLIFTING EXPERIENCE

No one would ever call Vasili Alekseev a small man. That's because he is 6 feet 1 inch tall and weighs 353 pounds. Alekseev has a 35-inch neck and a 60-inch waist. But he's not famous for his size.

Vasili Alekseev has been called the world's strongest man. In superheavyweight weight-lifting competition, the muscular Russian lifted 564½ pounds above his head. No one else has been able to touch Alekseev's record.

THIEF OF BAGS

Lou Brock (center) steals another base.

Lou Brock became a hero by stealing—bases. From 1965 through 1976 the St. Louis Cardinal star stole at least 50 bases a season. In 1974 he stole an all-time major-league record of 118.

Brock was also an excellent batter. In 1979 he became the fifteenth player in history to join the 3,000-hit club. Baseball's "good thief" finished his career with a total of 938 stolen bases—another major-league mark.

IRON MAN

A day of special tribute to Lou Gehrig

On June 1, 1925, New York Yankee Lou Gehrig went to the plate to pinch-hit. Although he made an out, it marked the beginning of one of the most unbeatable careers in baseball.

The next day Gehrig took over as the regular first baseman. He then played in every single game for nearly 13 years, a total of 2,130 games in a row. He took himself out of the line-up only after an incurable disease badly weakened him in 1939.

Gehrig's record may well stand forever. The closest that any player has come to the record is 1,307 games in a row. That's more than 800 shy of Lou Gehrig's magic number.

ESCAPE ARTIST

Master magician Harry Houdini was one of the greatest escape artists of all time. In 1903 Houdini was stripped, handcuffed, and bound at the legs, and then locked inside an "escape-proof" jail cell. It took him only 20 minutes to break out.

In London he accepted a challenge to escape from a special pair of handcuffs that had 6 "pick-proof" locks. Houdini managed to free himself in 1 hour and 10 minutes.

In 1906 he jumped into a river from a Detroit bridge wearing two pairs of handcuffs, and freed himself while still under water. Six years later he made escapes from straitjackets while dangling upside down high above the ground. No lock, restraint, or cell ever managed to hold the great Houdini.

WATER, WATER EVERYWHERE

Many people have sailed around the world. Some have even done it alone. But, until 1968, no one had done it single-handedly without stopping. That summer, ten sailors entered a contest hoping to be the first to succeed.

Nine of the contestants dropped out during the trip. Robin Knox-Johnston was the only remaining contestant after almost a year. The 30-year-old sailor covered over 30,000 miles before he docked his 32-foot yacht "Suhaili" in Falmouth, England. He had sailed around the world and had come back to his home port. It must have felt wonderful to be back because it was the first time he had set foot on land in 313 days.

WHERE'S FRIDAY?

Robinson Crusoe was modeled after a real person, sailor Alexander Selkirk. His ship was anchored to make repairs in September 1704 at a deserted island called Mas a Tierra, 400 miles off the coast of Chile. Selkirk quarreled with his captain just as the ship was about to leave. In his anger he demanded to be put ashore. His request was granted.

Selkirk was marooned on the island. He was able to survive by eating fish and turtles. Later he hunted goats. He made pets of the wild cats that roamed free, and used them to help control a booming rat population. He made clothing from goatskins and read his Bible to keep his mind alert. For more than four years, Alexander Selkirk lived entirely alone. In 1709 a passing ship saw Selkirk's signal fire and rescued him.

ONE THAT DIDN'T GET AWAY

Alfred Dean had a whopper of a fish story to tell on April 21, 1959. Near Ceduna, Australia, Dean reeled in a great white shark that weighed 2,664 pounds and measured 16 feet 10 inches—the largest fish ever caught with rod and reel.

UP, UP, AND AWAY

Fifty years after Charles Lindbergh's historic flight from New York to Paris, jet airplanes were crossing the Atlantic on regular schedules. But no one had traveled the distance in a balloon.

Three friends from Albuquerque, New Mexico, thought they could be the first ones to make the crossing. The first time they tried it, Ben Abruzzo, Maxie Anderson, and Larry Newman landed in the ocean.

They decided to try again. Early on the morning of August 11, 1978, their helium-filled "Double Eagle II" rose into the air from Presque Isle, Maine. As they drifted eastward, they were sometimes as high as 4 miles above the sea. It was very cold at those high altitudes in their small open gondola.

They traveled more than 3,000 miles in 6 days before they landed in a wheat field at Miserey, France. Their amazing Atlantic crossing set the world distance record for balloon flight.

FOLLOW THE CURRENT

The people of the Pacific islands of Polynesia were believed to have come from Asia many years ago. But a Norwegian scientist named Thor Heyerdahl thought differently. He knew that the legends of the Polynesians and Peruvian Indians spoke of a great leader named Kon-Tiki. Because of this similarity, Heyerdahl believed some Polynesians might have come from South America. He set up an expedition to demonstrate how they may have managed the trip.

Heyerdahl used balsa logs to build a 45-foot raft like the ones the Peruvian Indians might have used. He and a crew of five set sail from Peru on April 28, 1947.

The Kon-Tiki sailed 101 days and 4,300 miles before it reached the reefs of Polynesia. The voyage of the Kon-Tiki proved that Heyerdahl's theory was indeed a possibility.

OUT OF SIGHT

A glider

An expert West German pilot named Hans-Werner Grosse left Lübeck, Germany, in an airplane-towed glider on April 25, 1972. After the towline was released, he had to find currents of warm air to keep his engineless glider aloft. He hoped to break a record by gliding nearly 700 miles to the French town of Nantes. But the air currents were so good when Grosse reached Nantes, he decided to see how far he could go.

By the time he landed in the French town of Biarritz near the Spanish border, Grosse had spent 12 hours in the cramped cockpit of his glider. He had flown more than 900 miles—a new world gliding record.

SOARING SKIS

In March 1976 Austrian Toni Innauer made the longest ski jump ever recorded in competition. He sailed through the air 577.42 feet. That's nearly twice the length of a football field.

FLYING SKIS

Most people use their water skis in the water. But not Sammy Duvall of Greenville, South Carolina. In August 1979 he jumped 182 feet through the air on his skis—for an all-time record.

NO LIFT

Japanese skier Yuichiro Miura wanted to be the first man to ski at least partway down Mount Everest, the world's highest mountain. Getting Miura to Mount Everest was costly. It took the lives of 6 native guides and more than $3,000,000.

But Miura did achieve his goal 3,000 feet from Everest's peak. For about 2 minutes in May 1970, he skied down an icy slope 26,000 feet above sea level. No one has ever skied at a higher altitude.

UP IN THE AIR

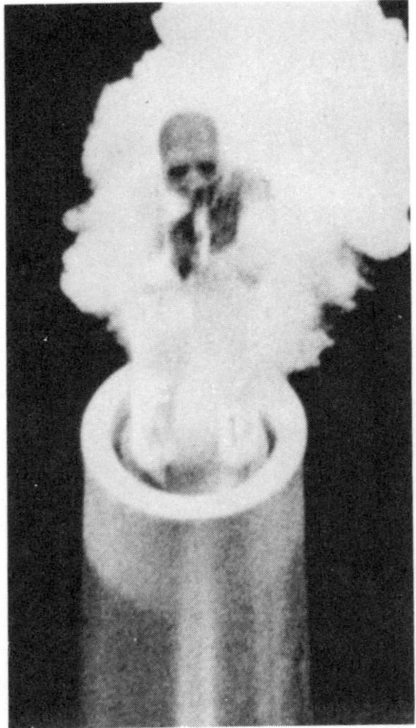

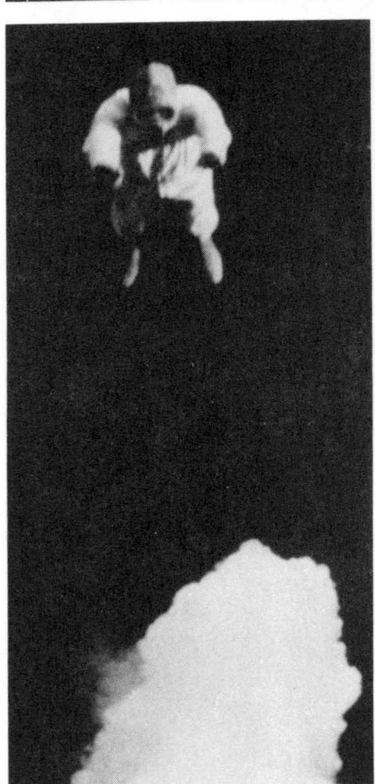

Hugo Zacchini had a unique circus act. He was the original human cannonball. With a flash of light and a puff of smoke, he would fly out of a huge cannon 75 feet into the air and land in a net more than 150 feet away. He performed his act hundreds of times in Europe and the United States between 1922 and 1961. Someone once asked him if he was ever frightened during his act. His reply? "It is nothing," he said casually.

PERFECT RECOVERY

Ben Hogan was the number-one golfer in the United States in 1948. He won the PGA (Professional Golfers' Association) tournament and the Western Open tournament, and he took the U.S. Open with a score 5 shots better than the old tournament record.

But in 1949 he was nearly killed in a head-on auto accident. The doctors were amazed that he had survived. Hogan wasn't content with just being alive. He painfully exercised his torn-up muscles back into shape. Within 4 months he began playing golf again.

He entered his first tournament 11 months after the accident. Hogan tied for first place but lost in the play-off. At the U.S. Open in June 1950 Hogan wasn't about to settle for second best. He finished in a three-way tie for first place, and won the play-off by 4 strokes. After his near brush with death, Ben Hogan was back, and better than ever.

ON THE WING

Hang gliding

George Worthington breezes through life, floating through the air with the greatest of ease. That's because he spends much of his spare time hang gliding. In July 1977 he set the world hang gliding record. He took off from Cerro Gordo Peak in California and swooped and turned for a distance of 95 miles. The next year he took off from the same place and made another world record when he gained 11,700 feet of altitude.

BUCKLE YOUR SEATBELT

A daredevil known as "The Human Fly" took an unusual airplane ride in April 1977. He stood on top of a DC-8 jetliner as it flew through the sky at more than 200 miles an hour.

THE BIRTH OF FLIGHT

Wilbur and Orville Wright

At the beginning of the twentieth century many people were trying to invent flying machines. The mystery of flight fascinated two bicycle mechanics named Orville and Wilbur Wright. The brothers spent six years building gliders and studying the principles of flight. In 1903 they took a very simple but specially designed aircraft to the sands of Kitty Hawk, North Carolina. It had a gasoline motor that powered a propeller.

Orville was at the controls on December 17 as the propeller slowly started turning. He released a wire that held back the plane. After speeding along a guide rail for 40 feet, the craft rose 10 feet into the air and flew for about 12 seconds.

Even though Orville flew only 120 feet, the flight was historic. A few people had already made short hops in powered aircraft, but Wright's flight was the first that the pilot had controlled.

By the end of that morning, the Wrights were able to keep their marvelous machine flying for a minute at a time. Then a sudden gust of wind turned it over and damaged it. That first plane never flew again. But the air age had begun.

AHEAD OF HIS TIME

Da Vinci's sketch of a helicopter

Leonardo da Vinci created two of the world's most famous paintings, "The Last Supper" and "The Mona Lisa." But the great Italian artist was so busy learning that he completed very few paintings in his lifetime.

Leonardo studied the way that light and shadow blend so that his paintings would be more lifelike. He studied the muscle and bone structure of humans and animals and made careful, detailed drawings of what he saw.

But more astonishing is the wide variety of the inventions he dreamed of. Leonardo's notebooks contain the earliest known diagrams for a parachute, a helicopter, a paddle-wheel boat, a self-propelled car, and many other advanced ideas.

These ideas were not practical in the late 1400s and early 1500s. Today they are a part of everyday life. Leonardo was a man whose ideas were hundreds of years ahead of his time and technology.

LUCKY LINDY

A prize of $25,000 was offered by a New York hotel owner in 1919 to the first aviator who could fly across the Atlantic Ocean nonstop between New York and France. Many fliers tried to claim the prize, and a few lost their lives in the attempt.

Charles Lindbergh was a flier with a dream. Early on the morning of May 20, 1927, he climbed aboard "The Spirit of Saint Louis," parked at Roosevelt Field on Long Island. He took along five chicken sandwiches and a canteen of water to last him through the flight. The specially built plane was heavily loaded with a huge supply of fuel for the long journey. On take-off, the wheels just managed to clear the telephone wires at the end of the runway.

Lindbergh's biggest problem on the flight was drowsiness. He found himself dozing as he reached the halfway point.

After 25 hours in the air, he passed over a fishing boat. Then he saw the coastline of Ireland on the horizon. Lindbergh was exactly where he'd planned to be at that hour.

When he landed his plane at Paris's Le Bourget airport, a cheering crowd greeted him. After 33 hours alone in the air, Charles Lindbergh had conquered the Atlantic.

SPACE WOMAN

Cosmonaut Tereshkova in training

A Russian cosmonaut named Valentina Tereshkova is the only woman to have traveled in space. On June 16, 1963, her "Vostok 6" space vehicle was rocketed to within 3 miles of the "Vostok 5," which had been launched 2 days earlier. Tereshkova orbited the earth 48 times during the three days of her flight. The 26-year-old parachute jumper had logged more than 1,000,000 miles by the time she landed safely back on earth.

CYCLE FLIGHT

In 1979 Dr. Paul MacCready built the human-powered "Gossamer Albatross" to fly the 21-mile English Channel. Its clear plastic wings stretched 96 feet from tip to tip. The entire craft weighed only 75 pounds. Its pilot and "engine" was biologist and bike racer Bryan Allen, who weighed about twice as much as the plane.

Allen sat down in the plastic cockpit on June 12, 1979, and furiously pumped the pedals that turned the propeller behind him. The plane took off from England, and headed for France.

Two hours and 49 minutes after leaving England, Bryan Allen brought the "Gossamer Albatross" down on a French beach. Like a giant sea bird, he had flown the English Channel—entirely under his own power.

GOING THE DISTANCE

How far has anyone traveled in an hour on a bicycle? Belgian Eddy Merckyx climbed aboard a special one-speed racing bicycle at the Olympic cycling stadium in Mexico City in October 1972, and pedaled as hard and fast as he knew how. Sixty minutes later, the champion cyclist had traveled 30.7 miles—nearly half a mile farther than anyone else had ever gone on a bicycle in an hour. "I feel over the moon with joy," exclaimed Merckyx.

SUPER WALKER

Long before the gasoline shortage, Edward Payson Weston was America's number-one pedestrian. He first became famous when he walked the 478 miles between Boston and Washington, D.C., in only 10 days. Weston was on his way to see Abraham Lincoln's 1861 presidential inauguration. He was too late to see Lincoln sworn in, but he did make it to the Inaugural Ball. He even had enough energy to dance!

In 1867 Weston won a $10,000 prize by strolling from Portland, Maine, to Chicago, Illinois, in only 26 days. Forty years later, he repeated the walk and bettered his time by 29 hours.

To celebrate his seventieth birthday, Weston decided to take his first coast-to-coast walk, from New York to San Francisco. It took him just over 104 days. But Weston wasn't satisfied with his time. The next year he marched from Los Angeles back to New York. The 71-year-old pedestrian set a new record of just under 77 days for the 3,600-mile walk.

SEE WHERE YOU'VE BEEN

On July 26, 1930, in New York City, James B. Hargis and Charles Creighton got into their car and set out for Los Angeles. There was nothing unusual about this cross-country trip, except that they were going to do it backward!

The car seat was at an angle and there was an extra-large rear-view mirror. And they had moved the headlights from the front to the rear. With their car in reverse gear, they were all set to go. But they almost didn't make it out of New York City. A taxi crashed into their car soon after they began, and dented their left fender. They were able to keep on going, and at 7 miles an hour they reached Los Angeles 19 days later.

They turned around and headed back in reverse to New York. The car's odometer had 16,000 miles on it at the beginning of the trip. But when they arrived at their starting point on September 8, it had rolled backward to 8,820.

Creighton and Hargis had gone 7,180 miles, all in reverse. They drove home to St. Louis in triumph—and in forward gear.

TEETH PULLING

John Massis of Ghent, Belgium, has a mouth worthy of note. Massis once pulled two 90-ton (180,000-pound) railroad cars more than 70 feet—with only his teeth!

THAT'S A MOUTHFUL

The last time Helen Bordeau of Ephrata, Pennsylvania, tried to tow a Volkswagen "beetle," she could move it only 9 feet. But that wasn't bad. She was 83 years old at the time, and she did it with her teeth!

PLAYER IN A RUSH

On November 20, 1977, Chicago Bears running-back Walter Payton was just getting over the flu. He wasn't feeling too well and the sportcasters didn't expect him to play a good game. But on the very first play he ran 29 yards against the Minnesota Vikings.

Payton didn't have a bad day after all. In fact, he ran a total of 275 yards. That's the most yardage that anyone has ever gained on the ground in one professional football game.

TRIPLE FAME

Big Cal Hubbard gives a teammate a lift

Very few people are elected to a sports hall of fame. But Cal Hubbard is a member of three of them. He was elected to the College Football Hall of Fame in 1962 for his achievements as an All-American tackle at Centenary and Geneva colleges in the 1920s. The Professional Football Hall of Fame honored him in 1963 for his ten years of outstanding play with New York, Green Bay, and Pittsburgh between 1927 and 1936.

Cal Hubbard retired from football, and went on to become a great baseball umpire. In 1976 he was named to the Baseball Hall of Fame. Cal Hubbard is the only three-time hall-of-famer in history.

HIGH JUMP

U.S. Air Force Captain Joseph W. Kittinger rode a balloon to a height of nearly 19½ miles above the earth on October 16, 1960. The air was so thin that Kittinger had to wear a special pressurized suit. He stepped out of the open gondola and hurtled through the air, while an automatic camera recorded the jump.

Eighteen seconds later, a parachute opened above him. It was a special chute that kept Kittinger from spinning as he fell, but did not slow him down. Half a minute after he made his jump, he reached a top speed of 614 miles per hour.

It took Kittinger 4½ minutes to fall nearly 15 miles. His main parachute finally opened when he was 18,000 feet above the ground.

The trip from the balloon to the sands of the New Mexico desert took Kittinger 8½ minutes. From a height of 102,800 feet he had made the highest parachute jump and the longest free fall in history.

1-2-3 PULL!

In July 1977 an Englishman named Bob Broadbere made the first and last parachute jump of his life. "It was a fantastic experience," he said.

It was also fantastic enough to set a record. At the impressive age of 85, Bob Broadbere had become the oldest parachutist of all time.

LEAP INTO HISTORY

With one amazing jump in the 1968 Olympics, Bob Beamon made a fantastic leap into the record books. On his first try in the long-jump finals, the tall New Yorker raced down the runway and flew into the air. He came down 29 feet 2½ inches from where he'd started. That was more than 1¾ feet farther than anyone had ever jumped before.

It was a once-in-a-lifetime performance. Beamon himself never again came within 2 feet of his record leap. And no one else since has managed to approach the mark he set that day in Mexico City.

OUT FOR A STROLL

Some people would rather walk than ride. John Lees is one of them. He holds the speed record for walking across the United States. In 1972 the 27-year-old Englishman walked from Los Angeles City Hall to New York City Hall. It took him 53 days, 12 hours, and 15 minutes.

HANDS DOWN

In 1900 Johann Huslinger decided to hike from Vienna to Paris. The 871-mile walk took him 55 days, because he did it the hard way—on his hands.

IN THE SADDLE

Steve Cauthen
on inside lane at the
Belmont Stakes.

In the winner's circle
at the Preakness Stakes

When 1977 began, Steve Cauthen had been a professional jockey for just 8 months. By the end of the year, the 17-year-old had set record after record and won horse racing's highest award.

Five days after his eighteenth birthday, Cauthen rode a colt named Affirmed in the Kentucky Derby. Alydar, another great horse, was favored to win. But Affirmed crossed the finish line first, to give Steve a belated birthday present—his first Kentucky Derby victory.

Could Cauthen and Affirmed go on to win the other two races of the Triple Crown? In the Preakness and the Belmont Stakes, Alydar tried to break Affirmed's winning streak. But both times Affirmed won by a narrow margin. Steve Cauthen became the youngest jockey ever to ride to a Triple Crown victory.

SHARP SHOT

Annie Oakley was the world's most famous sharpshooter. Annie's father died when she was young, and she helped support her family by hunting rabbits and quail. She was such an excellent shot by the age of 15 that she was able to outshoot professional marksmen.

Annie Oakley became a star with Buffalo Bill's Wild West Show in 1885. She could do all sorts of trick shots. From a distance of 30 paces, she could shoot a playing card in two—with the thin edge held toward her. She could hit dimes that had been thrown into the air, and she once shattered 4,772 out of 5,000 glass balls before they touched the ground.

When she was touring Europe, Kaiser Wilhelm, the emperor of Germany, lit a cigarette and asked Annie to shoot it from his lips. The Kaiser's aides were horrified, but Annie stayed calm. She stepped back 100 paces, took careful aim, and fired. She didn't miss!

LARGER THAN LIFE

Sculptor Korczak Ziolkowski began blasting and hammering away at the rock face of Thunderhead Mountain near Custer, South Dakota, in 1948. So far he has moved more than 5,500,000 tons of earth. His project is the world's largest sculpture.

The finished monument will be 563 feet tall and 641 feet long. It will show Sioux Indian Chief Crazy Horse riding a charging horse. The Chief's head will be 87½ feet tall. His pony will be so large that a five-room house could easily fit inside each nostril.

Ziolkowski will probably not be able to finish this mammoth sculpture in his lifetime. But he has prepared plans so that others can finish what he has begun.

THE BIG PICTURE

In the 1840s artist John Banyard created the world's largest painting. Its subject was the east bank of the Mississippi River. The canvas was almost a mile long!

How did Banyard display his enormous work? He rolled it up like a scroll, and unwound it from one end to the other in front of audiences who paid to see it.

Index

References to photographs are underlined.

Abruzzo, Ben, 60
Aldrin, Edwin "Buzz," 16, 16
Alekseev, Vasili, 53, 53
Ali, Muhammad, 51, 51
Allen, Bryan, 74, 74
Amato, Lorenzo, 4
Ammann, Othmar H., 10
Amundsen, Roald, 29, 29
Anderson, Maxie, 60
Armstrong, Neil, 16, 16
Atlantic Ocean, crossing, 12, 12, 60, 60, 72, 72

ballooning, 60, 60
Bannister, Roger, 36, 36
Banyard, John, 90
Barbe, Mrs. Jane, 20
Barbieri, Angus, 28
Barrett, Stan, 34, 34
baseball, 6, 50, 50, 54, 54, 55, 55, 81
Beamon, Bob, 84, 84
bicycling, 43, 75, 75
blind, Braille writing for, 23, 23
Blondin, 9
blood donations, 52
bobsledding, 49, 49
Bordeau, Helen, 79, 79
boxing, 49, 51, 51
Braille, Louis, 23
bridges, 10, 10
Broadbere, Bob, 83
Broadwick, Georgia Thompson "Tiny," 7
Brock, Lou, 54, 54

Cauthen, Steve, 86, 87, 87
Champollion, Jean François, 22
Chaplin, Charlie, 25, 25
chess, 41, 41
Christo, 3
climbing, 14, 14, 15, 15
Colcord, Harry, 9
Comaneci, Nadia, 47, 47
Coogan, Jackie, 25, 25
Creighton, Charles, 77

dancing, 46, 46
Dean, Alfred, 59
Didrikson, Mildred "Babe," 38, 38
dieting, 28
DiMaggio, Joe, 50, 50
diving, deep-sea, 27, 27
driving, 34, 34, 35, 35, 77
Duvall, Sammy, 64

Eagen, Eddie, 49, 49
Ederle, Gertrude, 11, 11
Edison, Thomas, 20, 20
Empire State Building, 31, 31
English Channel, swimming, 11, 11
escape artist, 56, 56
Everest, Mount, 14, 14, 65, 65
Ewry, Ray, 45, 45

Fischer, Bobby, 41, 41
fishing, 59, 59
flying, 37, 37, 60, 60, 62, 62, 68, 68, 69, 69, 70, 70, 71, 71, 72, 72, 74, 74
football, 80, 80, 81, 81

Gagarin, Yuri, 30, 30
Galilei, Galileo, 18
Gehrig, Lou, 55, 55
Gestring, Marjorie, 26
gliding, 62, 62, 68, 68
Goddard, Robert, 17, 17
golf, 38, 67, 67
Grosse, Hans-Werner, 62
gymnastics, 47, 47

Haegg, Gunder, 36
Hamilton, Charles Harold St. John, 21
hang gliding, 68, 68
Hargis, James B., 77
Heyerdahl, Thor, 61
Hillary, Edmund, 14, 14
Hillman, Harry, 39
Hogan, Ben, 67, 67
horse racing, 86, 87
hot dogs, eating, 5
Houdini, Harry, 56, 56
house of newspapers, 1
Howard, Edward "Spike," 52
Hubbard, Cal, 81, 81
human cannonball, 66, 66
"Human Fly," 69, 69
Huslinger, Johann, 85
Hutson, John, 35

Innauer, Toni, 63, 63

Jansky, Karl, 19
Jenner, Bruce, 44, 44

Johnson, Francis, 2, 2
Jones, Jackie, 21
Joyce, Joan, 6
jumping, 45, 45, 84, 84; see also parachute jumping; ski jumping
Jupiter's moons, 18, 18

Kittinger, Joseph W., 82, 82
Knecht, Richard John, 46
Knight, William J., 37, 37
Knox-Johnston, Robin, 57, 57
Kon-Tiki, 61, 61
Kuerth, Linda, 5, 5

Lees, John, 85
Leonardo da Vinci, 71, 71
Lindbergh, Charles, 60, 72, 72

MacCready, Paul, 74
Massis, John, 78, 78
Merckyx, Eddy, 75, 75
millionaires, self-made, 24, 24, 25, 25
Miura, Yuichiro, 65, 65
moon landing, 16, 16

Newman, Larry, 60
Niagara Falls, 8, 8, 9
Nicholas, Cynthia, 11
Norgay, Tenzing, 14, 14
North Pole, 13, 13, 29

Oakley, Annie, 88, 88
Oerter, Al, 42, 42

Pace, Darrell, 48, 48
parachute jumping, 7, 82, 82, 83
Payne, Andy, 33
Payton, Walter, 80, 80
Peary, Robert, 29
Pelé (Edson Arantes do Nascimento), 40, 40
Perkins, Frank, 28, 28
Petit, Philippe, 9, 9
phonograph, 20, 20
Piccard, Auguste, 27
Piccard, Jacques, 27
pizzas, 4, 4
pole sitting, 28, 28

radio telescope, 19, 19
Rafferty, Jim, 31
Reber, Grote, 19
Robertson, Lawson, 39
Robinson Crusoe, 58
Rodia, Simon, 1
Rosetta Stone, 22, 22
Rudolph, Wilma, 32, 32
running, 31, 32, 32, 33, 36, 36, 38, 38, 39, 39, 44, 44, 80, 80

sailing, 12, 12, 57, 57, 61, 61
Scott, Robert, 29
Selkirk, Alexander, 58
Shepard, Alan, 16
skateboarding, 35
skating, 43, 43
skiing, 65, 65
ski jumping, 63, 63, 64
soccer, 40, 40
South Pole, 29
space exploration, 16, 16, 17, 18, 19, 19, 30, 30, 73, 73
Spitz, Mark, 26, 26
Stare, J.C., 46, 46
Stenman, Mr. and Mrs. Elis, 1
Stewart, Mrs. Jean, 21, 21
strong man, 53, 53
swimming and diving, 11, 11, 26, 26

Taylor, Anna, 8
Telford, Max, 33
Tereshkova, Valentina, 73, 73
tightrope walking, 9, 9
twine, ball of, 2, 2

Uemura, Naomi, 13, 13

Vihlen, Hugo, 12, 12
Vesco, Don, 35, 35

walking, 9, 9, 31, 76, 85
Walsh, Donald, 27
water skiing, 64
Watts Towers, 1, 1
Webb, Matthew, 11
Weston, Edward Payson, 76
Willig, George, 15, 15
Wingo, Plennie L., 31
Wonder, Stevie, 24, 24
World Trade Center, 9, 9, 15, 15
Worthington, George, 68
Wright, Orville and Wilbur, 70, 70
writing, 21, 21, 22, 22, 23

Young, Sheila, 43, 43

Zacchini, Hugo, 66, 66
Zatopek, Emil, 39, 39
Ziolkowski, Korczak, 89